Don't Blame the Children

by Anne Schraff

Perfection Learning® Corporation
Logan, Iowa 51546

For information, contact:
Perfection Learning® Corporation
1000 North Second Avenue, P.O. Box 500,
Logan, Iowa 51546-0500.
Phone: 1-800-831-4190 • Fax: 1-800-543-2745
perfectionlearning.com

Paperback
ISBN-10: 0-7891-7537-1
ISBN-13: 978-0-7891-7537-3

Reinforced Library Binding
ISBN-10: 0-7569-8377-0
ISBN-13: 978-0-7569-8377-2

29997
3 4 5 6 7 PP 15 14 13 12 11 10
PPI / 5 / 10

1 EVERY DAY IN Ms. Elizabeth Finch's English 3 class, the same thing happened. Kathy Benedict liked English, especially now that they were reading works by modern authors. But Alec Ross always managed to mess up the class. He ruined it for everybody.

Kathy sat in her usual place and smiled at Todd Macon, her longtime friend. She looked at Todd again and she felt sad. As usual he had turned his burn scar to the wall. Kathy couldn't help wishing Todd didn't feel so ashamed of the scar.

Alec wasn't in class yet. That was unusual. "Wouldn't it be great if he didn't come today," Todd said.

Kathy nodded. Alec always came early. He wanted to begin causing trouble right away. He liked the class to be in an uproar as Ms. Finch came in.

But today when Ms. Finch came in, the class was quiet. She looked around in surprise. She seemed pleased when she realized Alec was not there.

The class went very well. Kathy couldn't remember the last time they had had such a good class. It was all because Alec wasn't there—laughing at people and making as much trouble as he could.

When the bell rang, Kathy and Todd walked out together. "I wonder where Alec is?" Kathy said. "He never misses class."

"Maybe he fell in South River," Todd said with a nasty grin.

"Don't say that," Kathy said. She was worried about Todd. He seemed to be growing more and more bitter. And he was still very self-conscious about the scar. He kept it turned away from view when he could. It was hard to tell if he was embarrassed about it or angry. There were days when he seemed mad at the world.

Kathy glanced over into the parking lot. "Hey, look, it's Alec's motorbike. He must be here."

Todd frowned. "Well, there goes

Vickers' history class."

Mr. Russell Vickers didn't let Alec cause as much trouble as Ms. Finch did.

But Alec managed to spoil the class somewhat. He always waited for somebody to make a mistake. Then he would try his best to humiliate the person who had made it.

Kathy and Todd sat down in their usual places in history class. The day was growing cloudy and dark. By nightfall it probably would rain. Kathy watched the door, waiting for Alec to come in. He usually kicked over a wastebasket to get the class laughing.

But Alec did not come and Mr. Vickers had started his discussion of the Abolitionists. "John Brown was an Abolitionist, a man who didn't believe in slavery. Some said that he was insane to do what he did at Harpers Ferry," Mr. Vickers said. "What do you think?" He looked out at the class.

Kathy liked Mr. Vickers. He had a fine voice and thick black hair. He looked like an actor and he was a very good teacher. He had come to Tyler High a year ago from Lancaster. He was a bachelor and he lived in the old Remington house. When Kathy looked at the old house with its twisted trees, she thought about *Wuthering Heights* and dark mystery.

"I think he was insane," Dee Loring said. "He belonged in a nut house for sure." Dee was a pretty but unpopular girl. She liked herself enough for ten people. That made it hard for anyone else to like her.

Mr. Vickers looked annoyed. "We don't use words like 'nut house' in this class."

Dee laughed. She seemed to miss Alec and his pranks. She didn't like school much. She liked anything that upset things at school.

"John Brown had a cause he believed in," Todd said, "and he did something about it. That isn't crazy."

"So you approve of what he did?" Mr. Vickers asked Todd.

"Maybe," Todd said. "It's like war. Sometimes you have to be violent.

Sometimes there isn't any other way."

The class discussion went on. Kathy kept thinking about Alec. Why wasn't he here? His motorbike was. She had a strange feeling that something had happened to Alec.

Alec was missing from Mr. Sonderville's chemistry class, too. Mr. Sonderville was a war veteran. He was somewhat deaf and Alec loved to make fun of him.

When Mr. Sonderville saw Alec's empty desk he smiled. "Good. Now we'll have a wonderful class."

Most of the students laughed.

At noon, a large group of students gathered around Alec's motorbike. Nobody had seen him since the day before.

"Maybe he didn't go home last night," somebody said.

"But where could he be?" a girl asked.

"Who cares?" Todd said. "Good riddance to him."

"I'm going to see what I can find out in the office," Kathy said.

"They won't tell you anything," Dee said. "They don't know anything. I called Alec's house. Nobody knows where Alec is."

There was a long silence. Kathy looked at Todd. She knew that Todd disliked Alec. He disliked all the kids like Alec, the troublemakers and hoods. Sometimes it scared her how much he disliked them. She thought it had something to do with his scar.

"It seems like a hole opened up and swallowed Alec," Kathy said.

Just then another of Alec's friends, Mike Perth, came up. "I hear Alec is missing. We got football practice this afternoon. I can't see him missing that."

"He's probably just playing a joke on everybody," Kathy said. "You know how he likes to worry people." She didn't know if she really believed that.

"What's everybody so worried about?" Todd asked. "The jerk is gone. So what?"

Mike looked at Todd. "He's a friend of mine, *scarface.*"

Todd turned and looked at Mike. "Nobody calls me that."

Kathy was frightened by the look on Todd's face. "Please, Todd, don't let him get you mad! What difference does it make what he says?"

Mike grinned. "Want to take me on, *scarface*?" He was taunting Todd on purpose. Mike was about twenty pounds heavier than Todd. He was sure he could beat Todd in a fight.

Everybody stepped back to make room for the excitement as Todd lunged at Mike. Kathy couldn't believe her eyes. Todd knocked Mike off his feet and the big senior fell flat on his face. Then Todd jumped on Mike's back. He jerked Mike's arm behind his back.

Kathy could almost hear Mike's bone crack.

"Want to say you're sorry? Or you want a busted arm?" Todd said.

"I'm sorry!" Mike almost screamed in pain.

"I don't hear you," Todd said, twisting

Mike's arm even harder.

Kathy stared at Todd. She had never known how much hate Todd had in him.

"I'm sorry!" Mike cried.

Todd let him up then. He looked at Mike and said, "Next time, I'll kill you."

Kathy felt numb. What was wrong with him? She had known Todd since they were in the third grade. For the past two years, they'd been dating one another. They told each other everything.

There was only one secret between them. Todd had never told her how his accident happened. He had gone away one summer and had come back a changed person. He had always been fun. Now he was cruel and angry. Kathy feared that the real scars were not on the outside. They were in his heart.

Kathy looked at Todd with disbelief.

"Don't start with me," he snapped at her. He turned and walked away.

"That guy is crazy!" Dee exclaimed. "A total maniac!"

Mike was rubbing his arm. "He ought to be locked up."

Tears filled Kathy's eyes. She stared at Alec's bike again and she wondered.

2 AS THE STUDENTS left Tyler High that afternoon, the police arrived. Kathy saw Mr. Vickers talking with two police officers. A light rain was falling and the wind was cold. Kathy heard a little bit of what they were saying.

"He wasn't very popular except with his crowd," Mr. Vickers said. "D student. Mostly a troublemaker. Parents spoiled him, I'm afraid. I think he just ran away. It would be like him. It would be a way of hurting his parents. He seemed to enjoy hurting people."

The police went to the principal's office next. Mr. Vickers buttoned up his overcoat and headed for his car. He saw Kathy and stopped. "Oh, Kathy. See you a minute?"

Kathy walked over.

"Your paper on Lincoln is very good. I've read the first draft. Excellent paper."

Kathy smiled. Mr. Vickers rarely praised anything. She felt really proud.

"Thank you, Mr. Vickers. I'll do even better on the next version."

"I expect that you will." He got in his car and drove south.

Kathy put on her raincoat and headed for her bike. The campus was almost empty now. She thought about Alec and felt cold in a way that had nothing to do with the weather.

Kathy always rode home past South River. Usually it was a pretty ride. The river was clear and blue when the sky was blue. But now the sky was gray. The clouds looked like dirty gray sheets. As a result, South River looked gray, too. It also looked menacing. Kathy tried not to look at it. The water was wild and choppy in the rain.

Kathy thought that maybe Alec was in that river. She wished that Todd had not said, "Maybe he fell in South River."

Kathy stopped at the library to do some research for class, then rode home. She found her mother in the living room.

"Oh, you're dripping wet, Kathy!" her

mother exclaimed. "Why didn't you call me or ask Todd for a ride?"

"Doesn't matter." Kathy tried to smile. "Oh, Mom, you know what happened at school today? Alec just disappeared—"

"Disappeared?" her mother said.

Kathy's father walked in and asked, "Who disappeared?"

Kathy explained to her parents what happened.

"I'm sure he just ran away," Kathy's father said. "That boy is a bad apple. I always figured he'd do something like this."

"Oh, his poor parents!" Kathy's mother said. "They must be worried sick. I hope nothing has happened to him. You know how he was always sneaking into South River for a swim. He didn't care about the 'No Swimming' signs.

"I'm worried. That river is so dangerous. They should have fenced it off years ago."

Kathy's father laughed. "Dorothy, Dorothy. Nothing has happened to the boy. Don't go thinking the worst."

Kathy smiled at her father. He had a way of making everything seem okay. She had been so worried, but now she felt silly. Of course Alec had just run away.

The next day was bright and clear. Kathy hurried to school on her bike. She was sure that by now Alec had been found. He had probably been hiding in somebody's garage. He wasn't brave enough to go far.

The motorbike wasn't there. "The police took it," Dee said. "They looked all through Alec's locker, too."

The old fear returned. Kathy looked at Dee. "I thought he'd be back by now."

Dee shook her head. "My mom called Alec's parents last night. They didn't have a fight with Alec or anything. They don't know what happened."

Kathy tried to remember the very last time she had seen Alec. It was the day before yesterday in Ms. Finch's class. He was cracking his gum all during class. Every time Ms. Finch turned to the board, he did it. That really made her nervous.

Alec loved to make Ms. Finch nervous because she made mistakes then. She had called Shakespeare "Shakespoor" and everybody had laughed.

"Didn't I fix her today?" he had said after class.

"That was really mean, Alec," Kathy had said.

"Ahhh—where's your sense of humor?"

"It isn't funny when you hurt someone."

"Finch bores me. I hate her class."

"All the teachers bore you, Alec."

He had grinned. "Yeah." And then he had walked away.

Kathy remembered then that she had seen him later. She had seen him after Ms. Finch's class.

It was right after school and he was running from the science building. He was laughing wildly.

"What happened, Alec?" Kathy had yelled to him, but he hadn't stopped. He just kept running.

Kathy wondered now what he had been doing in the science building.

Before going to her first class, Kathy went to the chemistry lab. Mr. Sonderville was making a chart of atomic symbols.

"Hello, Mr. Sonderville," Kathy said. She looked around the lab. She noticed that the mice cage was empty.

"Hello, Kathy. What can I do for you?"

"Mr. Sonderville, excuse me. But where are the mice?"

A shadow passed over the old man's face. Then he sighed and said, "Alec put a snake in their cage. He did it the day before yesterday."

"Oh," Kathy said sadly. She knew now why Alec had been laughing.

"Fed my mice to the snake," Mr. Sonderville said.

"I'm sorry. I know the mice were important to your experiments," Kathy said.

The chemistry teacher nodded. "I was sort of fond of the little creatures, too."

"I'm really sorry."

Then Mr. Sonderville said something that surprised Kathy. "That boy had better watch out—maybe someday somebody will feed him to something."

Kathy thought about what Alec had done to the mice. She wondered if maybe Mr. Sonderville had gotten so mad at Alec that he—

No! Kathy stopped herself. She was letting her imagination run wild. Yet— Kathy knew that Mr. Sonderville had suffered terribly when he was in the war. You could still see the pain in his face when he talked about it—which he rarely did. Maybe Alec's twisted sense of humor had upset Mr. Sonderville so much that he just went crazy and—

Kathy shook her head to drive the thought away.

At lunch, Kathy couldn't eat the sandwich her mother had packed. She couldn't eat anything.

Todd came over and sat next to her. He didn't say anything for a minute. Then he said, "Look, I'm sorry about yesterday. I didn't mean to yell at you."

"I know. It just scared me—how you hurt Mike."

"He had it coming," Todd snapped.

"I don't like to see you fight. I care too much about you," Kathy said softly.

Todd smiled and offered Kathy half his orange. She found she could eat that.

"Todd, what do you really think has happened to Alec?"

"I just don't think about it," he said. "I'm thinking about my biology test tomorrow."

"But you must have ideas," Kathy insisted.

"Maybe he made somebody mad and the—" Todd stopped himself.

"You know, he put a snake in with Mr. Sonderville's mice. He did that the day before yesterday."

Todd frowned. "Whatever happened to Alec, he had it coming."

Kathy touched Todd's arm. "You don't mean that," she said. She was sorry she'd told him about what had happened.

Todd slammed his biology book shut and stared into space.

Kathy looked up at the sky. It was blue and clear now. She remembered the many summers she had spent with Todd—talking and laughing.

It used to be that Todd could make Kathy laugh whenever she was in a bad mood. He always picked up her spirits. But he had changed so much.

Kathy looked at Todd's profile. He was very handsome. The scar was on the other side of his face. From this side he looked perfect.

The accident that had scarred Todd was the only secret between them. Todd would not talk about it. Kathy thought that maybe, if he talked about it, he would feel better.

"Todd, you seem kind of sad and bitter," Kathy said softly.

He didn't look at her. "I've got problems."

"Can't I help you? You always helped me when I had problems."

He turned toward Kathy. She could see the scar now.

"Look at me," Todd said, "and then tell me if you think you can help me."

"The scar isn't half as bad as you think it is," Kathy said. "And maybe you'd feel better if you told me about it."

Todd closed his eyes for a moment. Then he asked, "Do you want to hear how it happened?"

"I think it might help if you talked about it."

"It won't help. But maybe it will make you understand," he said. He made a fist with his right hand. He kept nervously pounding it into the palm of his left hand. "You see, that summer in Lancaster—I was just walking down the street and I heard a girl scream. I turned and I saw this car on fire. There was nobody around to help her. She was trapped in the car— the flames were all around her—"

"Was she a little girl?"

Todd shook his head. "No. She was about eighteen. She was pretty, real pretty. She looked something like you, Kath. I ran to the car. I opened the door to pull her out. And then the car exploded. It was the gas tank. It just exploded. I was thrown about twenty feet. When I woke up in the hospital, they told me the girl was dead."

"Oh, Todd—" Kathy said.

"I was burned and cut. The doctor said there would be scars on my face, my back, and my legs. But she was dead." He looked down for a moment. He said nothing at all. Then he turned to Kathy. "Do you want to know how the fire started?"

"Yes, if you want to tell me," Kathy said quietly.

"Some kid—it was a prank. He saw the girl sitting in the car. He threw a firecracker into the car. Some newspapers caught fire and then her clothes. Wasn't that some joke?"

"What a terrible thing," Kathy said.

"Yeah. Isn't that just like something Alec would have done? That's why I hate people like that. That's why I hate punks. Do you understand?"

"I guess so, Todd."

He stood up. "The girl was killed. And what about me? You know why I don't go swimming anymore? You should see the way the other scars look, Kath. You should see. They're even worse than the scars on my face. It was somebody's joke, Kathy. Somebody like Alec."

"Todd—"

"I got to go to biology now."

Kathy watched Todd walk away.

In the afternoon, the police began talking to students in the principal's office. A Lieutenant Dexter was in charge of the investigation. Kathy was in history when somebody brought a note calling her to the principal's office.

Kathy's legs turned to water. Why did they want to talk to her? She wasn't close to Alec. What could she tell them? Or did they want to talk to her about Todd? Did they suspect something?

Kathy almost stumbled on her way out.

3 LT. DEXTER INTRODUCED himself when Kathy arrived. He was a tall, thin man with deep brown eyes. He had thin lips. He seemed to be able to look right through you.

"You are Kathy Benedict?"

"Yes."

"Please sit down. I'm talking to students who had classes with the missing boy. Did you know him well?"

"No," Kathy said.

"But Tyler is a small school. You must have some idea of who his friends were. Perhaps you also know some people who didn't like him."

"Most of the kids didn't like him."

"Mmmm." Lt. Dexter stared at Kathy. "How did you feel about him?"

"I didn't like him either. He could be pretty cruel."

"Do you know anybody at school who might have hated Alec enough to harm him, Kathy?" Lt. Dexter seemed to be trying to smile. It wasn't much of a smile though. He made Kathy nervous.

"No."

"I see. Is there anything you might tell us that would be helpful?"

"I don't think so."

"All right then," he said coldly, "you may return to your class."

Kathy stood up. "Don't you think he just ran away? I mean—kids do that all the time—"

"You may return to your class, Kathy," Lt. Dexter said.

The next day they began dragging South River for Alec Ross's body. It was Saturday and a lot of people gathered on the river bank. Adults and children stood around talking and laughing. Some of the kids played ball and a few people had packed picnic lunches. Excitement was in the air. Nobody had ever disappeared from the town before.

Kathy hoped they wouldn't find Alec's body. She didn't like him, but she didn't want him to be dead. She couldn't stand to go to South River and watch the large machines work. So she sat in her room and worked on her Lincoln paper. And she prayed they wouldn't find Alec dead.

They didn't find Alec on Saturday. They found automobile tires and seats and all kinds of junk, but no body. Kathy was relieved. She was now more sure than ever that Alec had run away.

On Monday, Kathy sat next to Dee in Ms. Finch's class. "Things are sure dull around here since Alec left," Dee said. "Nothing to do but listen to Finch and her boring lecture."

Ms. Finch came into the classroom. She seemed in a fine mood. She really was a good teacher when the class was quiet. Dee made a face and dropped her heavy chemistry book. Kathy knew that Dee had dropped it on purpose. But when Ms. Finch looked, Dee said, "Oh, sorry, Ms. Finch."

Dee noticed another girl's stack of books perched at the edge of a desk. Dee managed to upset them, too, as Ms. Finch was making a point about Hemingway's stories. Some of the kids laughed. Ms. Finch seemed to be getting nervous and she stumbled over a word. "Just like old times," Dee giggled.

"Dee, stop it!" Kathy whispered.

"Stop it yourself, Miss Goody-two-shoes," Dee sniffed.

After class, Kathy said to Dee, "Maybe you don't have to pay attention in class because you cheat on tests. But some of us want to hear the lecture. We'd like to get something out of the class."

"Oh, Kathy, don't be such a jerk," Dee laughed.

"Well, you *do* cheat on the tests!"

Dee looked angry. "Don't you ever rat on me, Kathy Benedict. A girl tried to rat on me once and I took care of her. I taught her a lesson she'll never forget!"

"I'm not afraid of you," Kathy snapped.

After school that day as Kathy and Todd were walking toward the parking lot, Alec's mother drove up. Kathy said,

"Hello, Mrs. Ross. We're sorry about Alec. Have you heard anything?"

Mrs. Ross was a tall, pretty woman. Alec was her only child. She spoiled him. She let him do anything he wanted. Kathy expected Mrs. Ross would be terribly upset, but she was calm. "We haven't heard a thing. I'm sure Alec is all right though."

"Yes. I think so, too," Kathy said. "Do you think he ran away?"

"Yes, I'm sure of it," Mrs. Ross said. "Alec is a very sensitive boy. I think he's been hurt and now he's run away."

Todd came closer. "I don't get it, Mrs. Ross. What do you mean?"

"It's this school," Mrs. Ross said. "This is a poor school. We should never have let Alec remain here. He told us how bad the teachers were. He said he was terribly bored. I'm sure he just couldn't stand it anymore. My husband and I should have listened to the boy. He was crying out for help."

Kathy was amazed. "But Mrs. Ross, Tyler is a *good* school!"

"No, dear," Mrs. Ross said firmly. "At Tyler they simply didn't challenge Alec. He's a bright boy. Children who are very intelligent are often hurt by poor schools. I've read several books on the subject."

Kathy and Todd looked at each other.

Mrs. Ross went on. "The teachers at Tyler are inferior. For example, Mr. Sonderville is senile. A senile man should not be teaching."

Todd snapped, "Sonderville is a brilliant man. He writes for important scientific magazines."

"*I've* heard that he's senile. Alec told us that. And that Ms. Finch—Alec said she's not fit to teach. Her class is always in an uproar."

Todd laughed. "You should see how good it is with Alec gone."

Mrs. Ross said nothing. She coughed and then declared, "I'm here to see Mr. Hubbard, the principal. I'm going to tell him how I feel. I think the teachers at this school made Alec run away! Something must be done."

"Mrs. Ross, you got it all wrong," Todd said.

Mrs. Ross turned red with anger. She looked like a general leading her troops to war. "I'm going to ask that certain teachers be fired. There are going to be changes at this school. I think that Alec will come home then. He'll know that we finally heard his cry for help."

Todd and Kathy watched the woman hurry away.

"No wonder Alec is the way he is," Kathy said.

"Yeah," Todd said, "and now she'll probably scare Hubbard into firing some teachers."

"Mr. Hubbard wouldn't do that," Kathy said.

"Sure he would. He's not all that brave. Mrs. Ross is a big shot in town. She knows how to make things happen. She and her husband own the big plastics plant, don't they? Most of the people in this town work there. Mrs. Ross can have anything she wants, and she wants blood." Todd's voice was savage. "That jerk, Alec. He even makes trouble when he's gone!"

"Maybe Alec will come back before his mother makes any trouble," Kathy said hopefully.

"No, he won't," Todd said. Kathy wondered how he could be so certain.

"You don't know that for sure," Kathy said.

"Yes, I do. I sort of know stuff like that. I got a sixth sense or something. It's weird, but it's true."

"Todd, don't be ridiculous. Nobody knows things like that."

"I just wish they'd find the body before Mrs. Ross stirs up trouble," Todd said coldly.

"Todd, don't say that." Kathy felt ice cold.

"Why not?"

"Todd, sometimes I think there's something wrong with you. You say terrible things and you seem so angry. It bothers me when you act like that. I remember you when you were more understanding—"

"Things happened," he said, looking away.

"I don't like being with you as much anymore," Kathy said sadly.

"I'm sorry." He tried to smile. "Really I am. Okay?"

Kathy smiled a little. "Okay."

"It's just that I hate the idea of Mrs. Ross tearing this school apart. She could even make trouble for Mr. Vickers."

"Why him? He's the best teacher in the school. What can she say about him?" Kathy asked.

"Who knows? Alec didn't like him. And Vickers has had enough trouble."

Kathy stared at Todd and asked, "What do you mean?" Mr. Vickers' past was a big secret at school. Some of the kids talked about what a mystery man he was. Kathy didn't think anybody knew anything about him.

"Did you know Mr. Vickers before he came here or something?"

Todd looked nervous. "No—it's just— that summer in Lancaster, I saw him.

Nothing special. We just met."

"You said he's had enough trouble."

"Did I say that? Well, I just meant it seems like he's got a lot on his mind." Todd seemed like he was sorry he had said anything.

Kathy looked hard at Todd. "You know something about Mr. Vickers, don't you?"

"Please, Kathy. I don't want to talk about it."

"Is it something bad?" Kathy asked.

"No. I never should have said anything." Todd kicked a stone from his path. "Please, don't ask me about it."

"Okay," Kathy said, but she wished Todd weren't so secretive.

As Kathy pedaled home that day, she thought about the secret Todd couldn't talk about. She wondered if it had anything to do with Todd's accident in Lancaster.

Even after Kathy got home that night, more trouble seemed in store. When her mother got home from work, she said, "Jan Ross called me this afternoon. She asked your father and me to come to a parents' meeting tonight at the community center. I don't know what it's all about. But I said I would go."

"Oh, Mom," Kathy said, "she wants to make trouble for the teachers at Tyler. She thinks Alec ran away because he was bored at school."

Kathy's mother looked troubled. "Well, I thought I should go. After all, I've known her for a long time. I do feel sorry for her—with Alec missing."

"Can I come to the meeting, too, Mom?" Kathy asked. "I think somebody should be there to tell the truth."

Kathy's mother nodded. "I don't see why not. We'll have a quick dinner and then we'll all go."

Kathy's father didn't seem too happy about the idea. But he agreed to go along.

When Kathy and her parents arrived at the center, it was already crowded. Kathy saw Mike with his parents. He would gladly say terrible things about the school.

Then Dee and her parents came in. Dee came over to Kathy. "Well, are you here to stand up for these lousy teachers, Miss Goody-two-shoes?"

Kathy glared at Dee. She wished some other students would show up. Dee and Mike would both lie about everything.

But nobody else came.

4 MRS. ROSS BEGAN the meeting. "I want to thank everybody for coming. I know you are all just as upset as I am about conditions at our high school. My son even ran away because he was so unhappy there. Tomorrow it might be your children."

Kathy couldn't tell if most of the parents agreed with that or not. She thought maybe they had come just because they felt sorry for Alec's parents.

"One of the students is going to tell us how it is at Tyler," Mrs. Ross said. She turned to Dee and Dee jumped up. Dee loved to be in the spotlight. She wore a pretty new outfit and she acted very dramatic. Kathy thought Dee had probably rehearsed her speech—just as though it were an important part in a play.

"School is so terrible," Dee said. "Everybody's bored. The teachers don't do anything. They just read stuff out of books.

And the tests aren't fair. The teachers have favorites and pick on the other kids.

"Ms. Finch is one of the worst teachers there. She gets mad and screams and everything. Mr. Sonderville is really bad, too. He's senile. And Mr. Vickers flirts with the girls."

Kathy raised her hand. Mrs. Ross glanced at her but did not let her speak. Instead, Mrs. Ross said, "Mike? Do you have something to say?"

"Yeah," Mike said. "Dee is right. It's a lousy school. We got lousy books and lousy teachers."

There was nervous laughter at that. Kathy again raised her hand. Mrs. Ross pretended she didn't see it.

"My kid is getting an F in chemistry," one man complained. "Maybe that's because that Mr. Sonderville isn't any good. My kid is smart; I know that."

"Well," Mrs. Ross said, "Alec kept telling me how bad the school was. Now I realize he was crying out for help. I'm sorry I didn't listen."

Kathy waved her hand in the air. This time, she didn't wait to be recognized. "Mrs. Ross! All of this is unfair!" she shouted.

Mrs. Ross looked coldly at Kathy. "Now, dear, you're just too sweet to complain about Tyler High. That's very nice, but you have to see how the school is hurting other young people."

"But it's a good school!" Kathy said.

"Dee," Mrs. Ross said, "I believe you have more to say."

Dee stood up again. "Yes. I just want to say that all those terrible teachers should be fired."

Kathy spotted Mr. Hubbard then. He looked very nervous.

Just then, the door opened. Todd came in alone. He sat down in the back and listened for a while. Kathy hoped he wouldn't lose his temper and say something he would regret.

Mrs. Ross read a petition she had written to the group.

"We, the concerned parents and

students of Tyler High, demand that our school be improved. We demand that the poor teachers be fired. We demand a better program."

Todd stood up. "I've never heard so much garbage in my life."

Everybody began speaking softly. Mike jumped up. "That guy is nuts," he said.

The two boys looked at each other with obvious hatred. Kathy was afraid there would be a fight. But Mrs. Ross quickly began to pass the petition around.

"Look," Kathy's father said. "Look at them all signing it. Every parent whose kid ever got a bad grade is signing."

In the morning at school, Kathy could feel the tension in the air. Mr. Hubbard looked like he had seen a ghost. Twenty-five percent of the parents had signed the petition. Mr. Hubbard was so nervous, he almost ran head-on into Todd and Kathy as they entered the school.

"Look at him," Todd said bitterly. "He's ready to chop off some heads—just to please Mrs. Ross."

When they reached Ms. Finch's class, Kathy saw what Todd meant. Mr. Hubbard came in and sat in the back. He was obviously there to see if Mrs. Ross was right about Ms. Finch.

"Well, the moment of truth, eh?" Mike whispered to Dee.

Dee laughed. "Is it ever!"

Kathy looked at Todd. He just shook his head. He sensed it, too. Mike and Dee had a plot worked out.

Ms. Finch looked very pale when she came in. She obviously knew about the petition. She knew her job was at stake. She saw Mr. Hubbard sitting grimly in the back. He had come to judge her, and this class would be the courtroom.

"Today we are going to discuss Hemingway's short stories." Ms. Finch sounded really nervous. Kathy felt so sorry for her.

Mike raised his hand. "I want to ask a question about Hemingway." Mike never asked questions in class. He didn't care enough about any school subject to ask questions. Kathy figured he must have a bad reason for asking one now.

"Yes, Mike?" Ms. Finch said.

"It's about sex in the Hemingway stories," Mike said.

The class burst into laughter. Mike had asked the question just to throw Ms. Finch off.

Ms. Finch turned red. "I think—I think we should go on now—"

Dee's hand shot up. "I want to go to the bathroom."

"Well, Dee—yes," Ms. Finch said.

Dee tripped on purpose as she left her seat. She stumbled into Mike's desk and he said loudly, "Watch yourself, girl!"

Kathy looked at Mr. Hubbard. He was frowning and making a lot of notes.

"We are going to talk about Hemingway's stort shories," Ms. Finch said. She turned bright red. "I mean, short stories."

"Stort shories!" Mike repeated loudly. "Huh, what are they? I never heard of stort shories!"

There was an explosion of laughter.

Mr. Hubbard stood up. He clapped his hands together. "Let's have order in this classroom!"

There was immediate silence.

Kathy knew that Mike and Dee were trying to make Ms. Finch look as bad as they could. And they were doing a good job. Kathy spoke up quickly. "Ms. Finch, could you tell us about some of Hemingway's best short stories?"

Ms. Finch looked grateful. "Certainly, Kathy. One of Hemingway's early story collections—published in 1924—is *In Our Time.*"

Todd joined in. "Some people say his short stories are even better than his novels."

Kathy admired Todd for wanting to help Ms. Finch.

But Mike broke in with "Where were you in 1924, Ms. Finch?"

Ms. Finch turned red again. She was only in her early twenties. "In the book," she tried to begin, but Dee returned to the classroom at this point. She stopped at Ms. Finch's desk and asked, "May I sharpen my pencil?" She didn't wait for permission. She began loudly sharpening her pencil. Everybody started to laugh.

"Stop that!" Ms. Finch cried.

Dee smiled at the teacher. "Stop what? I want a nice sharp point. You know what good notes I take."

"Dee! You get back to your seat!" Ms. Finch shouted. She was almost hysterical.

Mike dropped his heavy biology book, making a loud noise. "Oh, sorry," he said.

Ms. Finch looked at him. "You're doing these things on purpose!" she cried. She rushed from behind her desk. In her nervousness, she knocked over her portable lectern. It fell to the floor loudly.

"Oh!" Ms. Finch sobbed. She put her hands to her cheeks. "Oh! Oh!"

Mr. Hubbard stood up. "This is shocking! I won't stand for this. I will suspend any student who dares to make another sound."

Ms. Finch looked as white as a ghost.

The rest of the class was like a nightmare. Nobody made any further trouble, but Ms. Finch made several mistakes. She was so shaken she stumbled over words. She repeated herself. She acted like someone who was half asleep.

When the bell rang, Todd walked back to Mr. Hubbard. "Mr. Hubbard, what you saw today wasn't the way it usually is. A couple of clowns tried to make Ms. Finch look bad."

Mr. Hubbard's eyes looked like glass. He said nothing and hurried away.

Todd slammed his fist into the palm of his hand. "He didn't believe me. Do you see what's happening? They got away with it, those idiots."

"Come on, Todd," Kathy said. "Let's get out of here."

"But don't you see?" Todd's eyes were wild. "They destroyed Ms. Finch. Those stupid jerks did that to her. And they're going to get away with it! Just like they always do." His voice was rising. Kathy was frightened.

"Todd, please. There's nothing you can do."

"Yeah, sure. Just let them get away with it, huh? Don't make waves. Let the jerks of this world do what they want. If they hurt somebody, that's too bad. Man, I'd like to push Mike's face in! I'd like to see Dee get what's coming to her, too!"

Todd's face was twisted with fury. His scar looked worse than ever. Kathy had never seen him so mad before.

"Please, Todd, calm down," she begged.

Todd turned and walked away. He stuck his hands in his pockets. His shoulders were hunched over.

Later in the day, Kathy saw Ms. Finch going to her car. Kathy ran to the teacher. "Ms. Finch, I'm sorry."

Tears were running down Ms. Finch's face, though she tried to smile. She dropped her car keys and Kathy picked them up for her.

"It will be okay," Kathy said. "Mr. Hubbard understood everything. I'm sure he did. You're a good teacher. I like your class a lot."

Ms. Finch mumbled, "Thank you," and got in her car.

Kathy watched the little red car drive away. Ms. Finch was a new teacher at Tyler. In fact, this was probably her first teaching job ever.

Ms. Finch had two kids to support by herself. It would be terrible if she lost her job.

Kathy told herself it would not happen. Surely Mr. Hubbard understood.

But then Kathy remembered the principal's angry glare. She couldn't kid herself. There was bound to be more trouble at Tyler.

5 THE NEXT DAY Mr. Hubbard sat in on Mr. Sonderville's class. Dee began to ask very hard questions. Kathy knew she was doing it to make Mr. Sonderville look stupid. But the questions were so hard that Dee didn't even ask them right.

"Your questions aren't making sense," Mr. Sonderville snapped.

"Don't you know the answers?" Dee asked. She looked around at Mr. Hubbard and smiled. She said very softly, "He's very old. He forgets stuff, you know."

"I heard that," Mr. Sonderville said, "and I want you to report immediately to the principal's office!"

Mr. Hubbard stood up. "Come with me."

That ended that. Kathy was happy that Mr. Sonderville, at least, had escaped the plot.

The newspapers carried stories about Alec Ross and the parents' group that day.

Large pictures of Alec appeared with a bunch of lies. "Look," Todd said, "they've written that Alec's a bright guy. They say he couldn't stand all the dull teachers!"

"That's a good picture of Alec," Dee said. "I wish they'd put my picture in, too. I could tell them plenty."

Kathy looked at Dee. "Yeah, more lies."

"Oh, shut up," Dee said. "I wish they would put my picture in the paper. I bet some talent agency would see it. I might get a TV offer or something. I know I look a lot better than some of those girls on TV."

Todd walked over. "Do you want to get your picture in the paper, Dee?" He had a nasty smile on his face.

"Sure I do. Why not? I have a lot to say about the school."

"Maybe you have to be dead before they put your picture in the paper," Todd said. He kept on smiling.

Dee glared back. "What a horrible thing to say!"

"Well, maybe Alec is dead. He might be in South River with all kinds of weeds.

Would you like to go there, too? Then you can have your picture in the paper, Dee."

"You're sick!" Dee yelled at Todd.

"Don't you think you're sick, too?" he shouted back.

"No!"

"What did Ms. Finch ever do to hurt you? Look what you did to her! What you did was rotten," Todd said.

"She deserved it. She's such a boring teacher!" Dee said.

"Well, Dee, look at it like this. Maybe all the jerks like you and Alec and Mike are heading for South River. Maybe there is some avenger who will just take care of you all," Todd said.

"An avenger?" Dee repeated. It was obvious that she didn't understand what Todd was getting at.

"Someone who will punish you jerks for all the rotten things you do," Todd said.

Dee looked at Kathy. "He's threatening me!"

"He's only joking," Kathy said. But she wasn't so sure.

"I'm going to tell the cops what you said!" Dee screamed.

"Go on. Tell them I'm the avenger of Tyler High," Todd laughed. But it wasn't a nice laugh. It was terrible.

Dee hurried away. She seemed really frightened.

"You shouldn't have said those things to her," Kathy said.

"Why not?"

"She believed you. Now she's frightened. She thinks you had something to do with Alec's disappearance. Who knows what she'll say about you?"

"I don't care. I hope she *is* frightened. Maybe she'll stop hurting people if she's frightened." Todd seemed pleased with himself.

"Todd, do you really think Alec is in the river?"

Todd looked at Kathy. Except for the scar, he was the handsomest boy Kathy had ever seen. Now he looked sinister. He looked like a stranger. Kathy was almost afraid of him herself. "Yes," he said.

Kathy felt like somebody had just poured ice water on her.

That night Alec's mother was on the local TV news broadcast. She talked about how bad Tyler High was. She showed pictures of Alec. Alec looked so nice in the pictures. The pictures made him look like any other boy. He looked harmless and friendly.

"Pictures lie," Kathy said to her mother. "None of Alec's meanness shows in those pictures."

"It's really strange that he doesn't come home," Kathy's mother said. "I can't imagine him staying away this long."

Kathy didn't say anything. She put on another sweater. It wasn't cold in the house, but she was cold. She kept hearing Todd's bitter voice. She kept hearing the funny way he had laughed.

Could Todd have killed Alec? The thought filled Kathy with horror. The old Todd she knew never could have killed anything. But maybe something had happened. Maybe Todd was sick. Maybe the accident had hurt his mind. Maybe he *was* an avenger.

Kathy cared so much for Todd. She felt she would die if Todd had hurt Alec.

The next day in Mr. Vickers' class, the subject of Alec soon came up again.

"Today we're going to talk about the vigilante movement that followed the Civil War," Mr. Vickers said.

"What's a vigilante?" somebody asked.

"Someone who takes the law into his or her own hands," Mr. Vickers said.

"There's a few of them in this school," Todd snapped.

A girl turned and looked at Todd. "What do you mean?"

Dee tossed her curly hair and said, "Never mind him. He's weird."

Mr. Vickers cut in. "I think Todd is referring to the way some of you acted in English class." Mr. Vickers had obviously heard the tale of Ms. Finch's distress.

"Finch isn't a good teacher. She shouldn't be teaching," Mike said.

"So you decided to take the matter into

your own hands," Mr. Vickers said. "And you were cruel and vicious in the way you did it. That's just how the vigilantes were."

"Somebody had to pay for the lousy way Alec was treated," Dee said. "All the teachers picked on Alec. They drove him out of school."

Mr. Vickers looked at Dee. "Are you sure of that?"

"Why, sure. Everybody says that," Dee replied.

"Are you sure Alec ran away?" Mr. Vickers asked again.

The students looked at one another.

"What if he didn't run away?" Mr. Vickers asked. "Let's suppose that he played a trick on somebody. Alec was always playing tricks. Maybe he played a trick on the same person one too many times. Maybe that person got fed up with it."

Mike looked nervous. Kathy wondered if Mike were thinking what she was thinking. Maybe there really was an avenger.

"You think Alec is dead?" Mike's voice was shaky.

"No, no," Mr. Vickers said. "I'm just supposing. But suppose he really didn't run away? That would mean that you hurt Ms. Finch for no reason at all. Do you see?" Mr. Vickers asked. He looked at the class. He had a strange smile on his face.

Dee was chewing her lip. She really looked frightened. Mike was frightened, too. They were Alec's best friends. Maybe they were his only friends.

At the end of the day, it was announced that Ms. Finch was not coming back. There would be a substitute teacher for English.

Dee smiled at Kathy. "You see? We were right. She was a bad teacher. Mr. Hubbard fired her."

Kathy shook her head sadly. "She wasn't a bad teacher. You made her look bad. You forced her to leave."

"We have the power now," Dee said. "Those teachers better watch out! If we don't like them, we'll just get rid of them. They just better watch out."

"You're disgusting," Todd said.

"What's a matter, Todd, jealous? We've struck a blow for student power." Dee laughed. She didn't seem frightened anymore.

"It was my idea, you know. I talked Mike into it. It was all my idea. I think I should be in the paper. I'm the one who got rid of dumb Ms. Finch. If Alec got his picture in the paper, I should, too."

"Maybe you'll get yours in the obituary column," Todd said.

Dee turned around. "What did you say?"

"I said, maybe you'll get yours in the obituary column! Sometimes they have pictures there," Todd said.

Dee drew back. "That's where they list dead people, isn't it?" Dee looked around for Mike and yelled, "Mike!" She spotted him by the window and went running over. Kathy saw her gesturing and glaring at Todd.

Kathy glanced at Todd. "Why don't you stop saying things like that? You'll just get yourself in trouble."

Todd shrugged his shoulders as if he didn't care. Sometimes Kathy had the terrible feeling that Todd didn't care about anything anymore.

That night at dinner, Kathy said to her parents, "I'm so worried about Todd. He's angry and bitter all the time."

Kathy's mother nodded. "I talked to his parents the other day. They're worried, too. Todd used to be quite happy. His mother told me he had been planning to join the swim team before the accident. He was a good swimmer. Todd even talked about winning some races— maybe going to the state meet. But he's so badly scarred now that he won't wear swim trunks or shorts or anything. He wants to hide the scars all the time."

"Can't the doctors do something?" Kathy asked.

"They did their best already," her father replied. "Sometimes you just can't make everything perfect again. Todd has to learn to live with his scars."

Kathy went into the den after dinner to

watch TV. She was studying for a history test and half watching a situation comedy. And then, suddenly, she heard a voice break into the comedy show.

"This is a news bulletin. Local police report the disappearance of another senior from Tyler High School."

Kathy almost dropped her history book. She stared at the TV screen.

"Dee Loring was on her way home from school today when she disappeared. She is the second student from Tyler to vanish mysteriously. Earlier, Alec Ross, also a senior, disappeared after school. He is still missing. We will report further details as they come in."

Then the TV show came back on the air.

Kathy sat there like a statue. She couldn't move. All the terrible things Todd had said pounded in her brain: *let the jerks of this world do what they want—maybe you'll get yours in the obituary column— maybe there is some avenger who will just take care of you all.*

"Mom! Dad!" Kathy cried.

Kathy's parents came into the den. "What is it, Kath?" they asked.

"They said on TV that Dee Loring has disappeared."

Her mother's eyes grew very large. "Oh, dear Lord—someone must be doing it, Kathy. There must be some madman who is taking those poor children."

Everything got black in front of Kathy. She thought she was going to faint.

6 AT SCHOOL THE next day, all the kids seemed worried. Most of them had thought Alec had run away—that is, until Dee disappeared, too. Now most of them were sure something terrible had happened to Alec. And that it had happened to Dee, too.

A cool, misty rain was falling, making the day even darker. As Kathy stepped inside the building and removed her soaking coat, she saw Todd. He certainly didn't seem upset, she realized. He even smiled when he saw Kathy. "How are you doing today?"

"Todd, haven't you heard about Dee?"

"Oh, yeah. I heard something about it. I guess she ran away, too, huh? Now she'll get her picture in the papers."

"Todd, something has happened to her!" Kathy cried.

"I don't think so," he said very calmly. "She was mad because Alec was getting all the attention. Now she's run away. She just wants to be on TV. She thinks some talent scout will see her picture."

Kathy was amazed at how calm Todd seemed. Everybody else was worried. Kids were saying things like, "Who'll be next?"

But Todd didn't seem worried at all.

"You really don't care if something has happened to Dee, do you?" Kathy asked him.

"Do you want my honest answer? Or do you want me to lie to make you feel better?"

"I already know your answer," Kathy said sadly.

Todd paused in the hallway at his locker. His eyes were dark and cloudy like the sky.

"I saw her burn to death," he said.

"You what?" Kathy asked.

"The girl in Lancaster."

"Oh."

"I'll never forget that. Never in a million years."

"It wasn't Alec's fault. It wasn't

Dee's fault," Kathy said. "They weren't even there."

"Sometimes I dream about her. I get mixed up in my dreams. She looked like you, Kath. In my dreams I think sometimes that *you* are in that car. You're the one screaming. There are flames all around you. I'm trying to save you, but I can't. I wake up in a cold sweat."

Tears filled Kathy's eyes. "I'm sorry."

"Sometimes the faces all run together. I see that girl and I see you. It's like one person. And the other faces run together, too. I see Alec and Dee and Mike and that punk who threw the firecracker—like one person. I hate them all."

"What happened to the guy who threw the firecracker?" Kathy asked.

"He ran away," Todd said.

"You mean they never found him?"

"He left town. I don't think they ever found him."

Kathy wondered if the boy had disappeared like Alec. She wondered if he'd really run away.

"He probably felt bad about what he did," Kathy said. "Surely he hadn't meant to kill somebody."

"He didn't care. That kind never cares."

On Saturday, Kathy asked her father if she could take the car and drive to Lancaster. "I have to find some answers, Dad."

"Well, that's a long drive," he said with a frown.

"I know, Dad, but it's important."

"I guess you can go then," Kathy's father said with a smile.

It was a two-hour drive to Lancaster. When she got there, Kathy first stopped at the newspaper office and asked to look at old newspapers. It had been two years since Todd's accident.

A clerk in the office showed Kathy to a microfilm-viewing machine. "All the newspapers are right here," she said.

Kathy quickly found the papers from the summer she was interested in. But she had to look for about twenty minutes before she found the headline: BOY

CRITICALLY BURNED IN VAIN ATTEMPT TO SAVE GIRL.

Kathy read the story eagerly, scanning it for some clue to help her understand Todd's bitterness.

Todd Macon, 15, is in critical condition at Community Hospital as a result of burns he suffered while trying to pull 18-year-old Diane Rawlins from her burning car. Macon was walking along Vine Street when he saw the Rawlins car burst into flames. Police said the car exploded before Macon could pull the girl to safety.

The victim, Diane Rawlins, was a recent graduate of Evergreen High where she had been valedictorian of her class. At the time of her death, Rawlins was an honor student at East County Community College and engaged to be married in June.

Police reports indicate a juvenile may have thrown a firecracker into the open window of the Rawlins car only seconds before the fire broke

*out. Police theorize sparks from the
firecracker ignited newspapers in the
backseat. The fire then spread quickly
through the car, reaching the gas tank
and setting off the fatal explosion. It
is believed that Rawlins was trapped
in the car by the flames.*

*No arrests have been made.
However, police said that a youthful
suspect had been questioned and then
released into his parents' custody
pending further investigation.*

Kathy was trembling as she finished
the article. She remembered first hearing
about Todd's accident two years ago. She
had sent him cards and flowers. She baked
a welcome-home cake for him when he
returned to town three months later.
He had looked the same, except for the
scar on his cheek. But he was different.
Something inside him had changed.

Kathy read more articles. They told
of Todd's improved condition. A lot had
been written about Diane. The stories
featured pictures of her from her high

school annual. She looked beautiful with her long, wavy hair and big eyes. Kathy did not think herself nearly as pretty. But she did notice a resemblance between Diane and herself.

One story told about Diane's funeral. The high school principal had given a eulogy. He listed the organizations Diane had belonged to and said that she was a very generous person.

Kathy called home and told her father briefly what she had discovered. Then she added, "Dad, I need the car for a little longer. See, I'd like to visit her family. I found out from the phone book that they still live here in town."

"Kathy, they might not want you to come," her father said. "Maybe they don't want to think about the accident. Maybe you'll just stir up sad memories."

"I could go there and ask them. If they don't want to talk to me, I'll go away."

"Okay," he said.

Kathy drove to a small brick house two miles out of town. A tired-looking man answered the door. He was about fifty years old, but he looked much older. "Yes?"

"Mr. Rawlins?"

"Yes."

Kathy swallowed and said, "I'm a good friend of Todd Macon's. Could I talk to you for a few minutes?"

His face softened. "Todd Macon—he was the boy who tried to save Diane. Yes, of course. Come on in."

The living room was dusty and messy. "You must excuse me. I don't keep a very tidy house," the man explained. "Not since my wife died. She's been gone a year now."

Kathy sat down in a straight-backed chair. "I just wanted a few minutes with you."

"Sure. By the way, how is Todd? Fine boy. A lot of courage, that one."

"He's okay, Mr. Rawlins. He'll graduate in June."

"Time moves along. Seems only yesterday that my girl was starting high school. Seems only yesterday that she and my wife were painting Diane's room— redoing it all." He got a faraway look in his sad eyes. "Seems only yesterday, and now both of them are dead."

"I'm sorry," Kathy said. "Mr. Rawlins, I don't want to bring back painful memories, but I wondered if you remembered the name of the boy who threw the firecracker into Diane's car."

"Why would you want to know?"

"It's hard to explain, Mr. Rawlins. See, sometimes Todd is very depressed about his scars and everything. He still thinks about your daughter a lot. He told me how beautiful she was and how he tried to save her. I just wondered if I could find out what happened to the boy who did it. You see, Todd thinks the boy was never punished. I thought maybe he would feel better if he knew that justice was done."

"Name was Elton Leach. Was always a bad one. Tormenting cats, throwing stones at windows. Always a bad one."

"Do you know where he is now?"

The man shook his head. "The police talked to him. Let him go home with his parents. Said he had to report to the juvenile court later on. He never showed up. His parents said he ran away to California.

"I don't know. I just don't think about it. For a while I wanted to kill him. It wouldn't bring my girl back though. I don't think about him much anymore."

"I understand," Kathy said.

"Some folks said he mighta drowned himself," Mr. Rawlins said.

Kathy grew stiff.

The man's voice continued, "My girl's boyfriend said he hoped that's what happened. The boyfriend said he hoped that Leach drowned himself. He was pretty tore up by the thing.

"I went down to the river after Leach disappeared. God forgive me, I guess I wanted for him to be in there." The man shook his head.

"Your daughter's boyfriend—was he somebody she knew at college?"

"No. She was engaged to a young high school teacher. He taught at Lancaster High. They met in a night class at college." Mr. Rawlins smiled a little.

"They were a handsome pair, those two. Would have had sweet children. My wife always said that.

"Poor fella. He had a nervous breakdown when Diane died. He was in a hospital for a while. Lost his teaching job. Don't know where he's at now. Very sad. The whole thing is very sad."

Kathy got up. "I really want to thank you for talking to me."

"No trouble. You say hello to Todd for me. He's a fine boy."

"Yes." Kathy turned once more. "I believe that your daughter is happy in another life, Mr. Rawlins. I believe very much that people don't just die and disappear."

"I thank you for those kind words, child," the man said. His eyes seemed wet. In another minute he would be crying. Kathy hurried out to the car.

Kathy had one more stop to make: Evergreen High School. She felt the rest of the story was there.

She drove to Evergreen High and went into the office. "I wondered if I could look through copies of your old annuals?" Kathy asked the woman in the front office.

The woman handed Kathy a stack of books and Kathy quickly found the one she wanted. She flipped through the pages for Diane's picture. The caption under the picture read: *student council president, big eyes, summer at the beach, Rusty*

Kathy returned to the school secretary. "I wonder if you remember this girl?" She showed the picture to the woman.

She smiled. "Oh, yes. Everybody knew Diane." She looked sad then. "You know about the tragic way she died, don't you?"

"Yes."

"Oh, she was active here. We have a small school, you know. Somebody like Diane really stood out. Was there something you wanted to know about her?"

Kathy said, "I don't suppose you could tell me who Rusty was? Do you see the name under the picture?"

"Oh, yes. Of course. The young teacher she was going to marry. He was five years older than she was, but she was so mature. He had graduated from Evergreen High, too, but that was before I worked here. Would you like to see his picture in the annual for his year?"

Kathy's heart was pounding. Somehow she had a feeling that Rusty was an important piece in this strange jigsaw puzzle.

"Right here," the woman said eagerly. "Here's the book we want." She seemed very interested in rediscovering old memories.

Kathy looked at the picture of a serious young man with thick, dark hair. He looked a lot different now, but in many small ways he was still the same man.

"That's Russell Vickers, my history teacher," Kathy gasped.

The woman said, "Russell, yes, that's his name. They always called him Rusty." She looked at Kathy. "Are you all right, dear? You seem very upset. You aren't going to be sick, are you?"

"No. Thank you," Kathy said. She turned and walked out into the sunlight.

Now she knew Russell Vickers' secret. A prankster had killed his girlfriend. Mr. Vickers had every reason to hate pranksters like Alec.

Like Todd, Mr. Vickers had good reason to want revenge.

7 LATER THAT DAY, Kathy told her father about the rest of her discoveries in Lancaster.

"It's so scary, Dad. That Elton Leach disappeared. Now Alec and Dee have disappeared."

They were driving along the river on the way home after Kathy had picked up her father at the workout gym. Kathy looked at the broad, silver river. Another storm was coming up. The wind made the river rough. It looked angry and dangerous.

Kathy shivered inside her coat and wondered what secrets the river knew. Did it carry in its stormy bosom the fates of three people? Is that where they had all disappeared to—Alec, Dee, and Elton? And who had sent them there? What avenger was to blame?

Kathy used to love the river. Now she hated to look at it. She felt as if she could almost see their faces.

"Where does the river end, Dad?"

"Do you remember the stories I told you when you were little? I said the river ran into a dark green woods. I told you every night the moon witch spread her starry cape. And then the waters flowed up into her hands. Then, in the morning, she opened her cape and the waters ran back."

"I remember, Dad."

Kathy wished she were little again. She wished she could worry about the moon witch once more. She did not want to be seventeen and worrying about three people who quite possibly were dead.

"I've seen where the river ends," Kathy's father said. "It flows into a large lake— Clear Lake."

Kathy said nothing. She wondered if that was where Alec and Dee had gone. To the end of the river.

On Monday, gloom hung over the school. It was as if a huge gray cloud cast its shadow over everyone. Nobody wanted to go to classes. It seemed foolish to study history and chemistry when people were disappearing.

Mike Perth seemed especially upset.

"I don't understand what happened to Dee," he kept saying over and over.

"She just wants to get her name in the papers," Todd said.

Mike glared at Todd. "She wouldn't run away like that. She would have told me. She always tells me everything."

"Did Alec tell you he was running away?" Kathy asked.

Mike frowned. Then he turned around and hurried away. Kathy looked at Todd and whispered, "He thinks he's next."

A red-haired girl, standing nearby, overheard. "Alec and Mike and Dee always caused a lot more trouble than everybody else. Maybe there is something to it. Maybe there's some spooky thing going on. All the troublemakers are slowly disappearing."

"Sounds good to me," Todd said.

The red-haired girl giggled. "Hey, Mike," she shouted. "Are you really going to be number three?"

Mike's back was turned. He looked around. "What?"

"Are you going to be number three?" the redhead repeated.

A tall, thin, lanky boy joined in. "Number three, Mike."

Mike was shaking uncontrollably. It was as if a strong wind gripped him and Kathy could only watch.

The substitute teacher in Ms. Finch's class was a mature, gray-haired woman. She wore a gray suit. Even her face seemed gray. "I understand this is a problem class. Well, I do not intend to have any problems. I am Ms. Etheridge and I will not take any foolishness from anyone."

At the end of the period, Ms. Etheridge assigned a three-page essay on Hemingway. Everybody groaned. Mike muttered, "I can't do three pages!"

"What was that?" Ms. Etheridge looked right at Mike.

"Uh—nothing."

"Good," Ms. Etheridge snapped.

All the students rushed out after the bell.

"Man, oh, man," a girl moaned, "why did

we make it so hard on Finch? Now look what we got!"

"Yeah," a boy glared at Mike, "it's your fault!"

"It was Dee's idea," Mike said. "I didn't want to do it. Dee thought it up. It wasn't my idea!"

"Etheridge is just what you deserve," Todd said. "Serves you all right for what you did to Ms. Finch."

"Couldn't we get Finch back?" a girl asked.

"After what you did?" Kathy said. "No, she'd never come back here."

Kathy had lunch under a tree with Todd. "I did something Saturday that will probably make you mad."

"Yeah?"

"I went to Lancaster and read about your accident in the newspapers. I found out who threw the firecracker and all about Diane Rawlins. And I found out about Mr. Vickers."

Todd said nothing for a minute. Then he spoke very slowly. "Don't tell anybody around here about Mr. Vickers. You know what would happen."

"I won't tell anybody."

"Mr. Vickers loved her a lot. He came to see me in the hospital to thank me for what I tried to do. He broke down and cried that day. I felt sorry for him. When he came here to teach, I promised him I'd never say anything about Lancaster.

"See, the punk—Leach—he disappeared and some people thought he had been killed. Mr. Vickers said some pretty wild stuff after the accident. I think the police in Lancaster thought he maybe had something to do with Leach's disappearance. They could never prove anything."

Kathy looked into Todd's eyes. "What do you think?"

"Mr. Vickers wouldn't hurt anybody," he said. He sounded almost angry. Kathy wondered if he were trying to make himself believe it.

"Do you think Elton Leach is still hiding somewhere?" Kathy asked.

"I figure maybe he's dead." Todd's hands

were tightened into fists again.

"Maybe he went into the river, too, like Alec," Kathy said.

Todd's eyes narrowed. "What is that supposed to mean? Do you think I had something to do with his disappearance?"

"No," Kathy lied.

"I was out of the hospital when Leach disappeared. The police in Lancaster talked to me. The police also talked to me here at school about Alec. They can't prove anything. They would probably like to though."

Kathy's mouth was almost too dry for speech.

"You didn't do anything," she said finally.

"That's right," Todd said.

All during chemistry, Kathy's mind wandered. She thought about the summer before Todd's accident. She and Todd had gone swimming at Gretchen Lake. Todd was showing off his diving from the high board. Kathy remembered how Todd had looked. He had seemed just like Michelangelo's statue of David.

Kathy had worn her new swimsuit for that date. Todd had grinned at her and said, "Hey, you look nice."

Kathy had felt a little embarrassed and yet pleased at the same time.

It was the last really good time they had had together.

In the afternoon, there were police cars all over the school parking lot. Kathy's heart almost stopped when she couldn't find Todd. She waited at Todd's truck for about twenty minutes. Finally, he showed up, whistling with his hands in his pockets.

"Oh, Todd, I was so worried. I thought you were talking to the police."

"Everything is okay," he said.

"Were you talking to them?"

"Yeah. They just wanted to know when I saw Alec last. They're talking to just about everybody again."

"Why?"

"I don't know. I guess they haven't turned up anything and they want to recheck everyone's story. They're talking to the teachers, too. I saw Sonderville and Vickers waiting to talk to them. Hey, Kath, want a ride home? I'll throw your bike in my truck."

"Okay."

Kathy climbed in beside Todd. She wished she could just drive on and on. She sat close to him and put her head back. The wind coming in the window felt good on her face.

"I feel sorry for Alec's and Dee's parents," Kathy said. "They must be so worried."

"Too bad they raised kids like that," Todd said.

"You have to feel sorry for them anyway," Kathy said.

"I remember when I was a little kid. Mom invited Dee to my birthday party. Dee wanted more ice cream. When she couldn't have more, she smashed her bowl. She ruined the party for everybody. I remember her mom saying, 'Oh, poor Dee. All this excitement must have tired her out!'

"Reminds me of a poem I read once. It went

Don't blame the children, whatever you do.
Don't blame the children, their world is so new.
Let them be free and let them explore.
Let them do whatever they want—and more.
And if they want guns and powder as well,
Let the dear children blow us all into—"

Todd stopped and smiled. "Catchy, isn't it?" Kathy shook her head and didn't reply.

They stopped at Kathy's house. "Want to come in for a piece of cake?"

"Sure. Sounds good."

Nobody was home when they went into the kitchen. Both her mother and father were still at work.

Kathy cut a big slice of cake for Todd.

"Great," he said.

Kathy smiled. "Thanks, I made it."

The front door opened then. Kathy's mother came rushing into the kitchen. "Have you heard the news?"

"Heard what, Mom?" Kathy's breath caught in her throat.

"They found Alec Ross!"

"Oh, Mom—"

"He was in the river," Kathy's mother said. "Miles from here. The current took him farther than they thought to look. That's why they didn't find him when they dragged the river."

"He was in the river," Kathy repeated. Somehow she had known he was. She hadn't wanted to believe it, but she had known. She looked at Todd to see how he was taking the news. She remembered his first reaction to Alec's disappearance: *Maybe he fell in South River.*

"A fisherman found him," Kathy's mother murmured.

"Mom, did they say he drowned? I mean, what did you hear?" Kathy asked.

"What?" her mother asked. She was still deep in her own troubled thoughts.

"Did he drown? Was it an accident, Mom?"

"I just heard on the car radio that they found him. Oh, his poor parents. Of course he drowned. He must have gone swimming in the river like he always did. He knew he wasn't supposed to. The river is so dangerous in places. He must have gone swimming and drowned. What else could have happened?"

Kathy looked at Todd. It had been a cold, rainy day. Why would Alec have left his bike at school and suddenly gone swimming in South River? It didn't make sense.

Todd said nothing. He reached up and touched the scar on his cheek. Then he dropped his hand. Kathy wished he would say something—anything. She wished he would say he was sorry to hear that Alec was dead.

But Todd said, "I'll put the cake away. It's too good to leave it standing out."

8 THERE WAS A large picture of Alec Ross in the morning paper. Alec was actually an ordinary-looking boy. However, they used his senior class picture, and in that picture he looked quite handsome. All the seniors looked pretty good in their class pictures. Alec's face was turned to one side. He looked like he was staring off into the distance.

The newspaper story said many nice things about Alec. It said he was a good student and that he was a talented athlete. None of it was true. He was not a good student and he was below average in sports. The worst lie though was that he was well-liked.

"I remember when he was born," Kathy's mother said sadly. "I remember how happy his parents were. It must be so terrible for them."

Kathy couldn't eat breakfast. She could only drink a little orange juice. She picked up the newspaper and tried to read, skipping over the stuff about what a good kid Alec had been.

"Listen to this, Mom," she said as she began to read aloud.

The body of 17-year-old Alec Ross was discovered among the willows near Lever Point by a local fisherman, Clyde Jornung. Ross, missing for over a week, apparently fell or was pushed into South River and carried downstream by swift river currents.

The discovery of Ross's body puts an end to rumors surrounding the boy's strange disappearance. At first it was believed young Ross had run away to protest conditions at Tyler High School. The boy's parents, believing that Alec was hiding because he disliked teachers at his school, organized a drive to rid Tyler High of poor teachers. One teacher has already been forced to quit in the wake of protests lodged against the school.

The police reported that Ross's body was fully clothed. They used this fact to discount theories that the boy was swimming before his death. However, police Lt. Dexter refused to comment on the time or cause of death, saying only that an autopsy would be performed to determine whether the drowning was accidental or not. "Due to the enormous public interest in this case," Dexter said, "autopsy results will be televised live in a coroner's news conference."

There was a picture of Dee Loring in the article, too. She was beautiful, and the picture made her look even more so. Kathy read the information about her.

Police would not comment on any connection between the disappearance of the two Tyler High seniors. When reached for comment, Jed Loring said he feared something terrible had happened to his daughter.

"It's all so horrible," Kathy said.

"It must have been an accident," her mother insisted. "Nobody in this town would have harmed Alec. How can the papers suggest such a thing?"

"But he didn't go swimming," Kathy said.

"He must have fallen in the river. He must have been down there for some reason and slipped and fallen in."

"Mom, Alec was a pretty good swimmer," Kathy said.

"He probably struck his head when he fell in. I don't care what anyone says. Those newspapers want to believe the worst. Murder sells newspapers. Nobody in this town would have hurt Alec. I don't care if he was a troublemaker. The people in this town are not murderers!" Kathy's mother insisted.

Kathy remembered Alec and thought about all the years she had known him. All that she could recall were bad things. Alec even played nasty tricks on his friends.

For instance, Mike Perth had a younger sister. She had a bad acne problem. Alec had made fun of her because of that. Even Mike, who was mean enough, had been bothered when Alec made his sister cry. It seemed like Alec was cruel to everyone.

Kathy thought about Mr. Sonderville and what he had said: *Maybe someday somebody will feed him to something.* Maybe Mr. Sonderville pushed Alec into the river. Maybe he wanted to feed Alec to the fish in the river!

Or perhaps that afternoon, Alec had played one final prank on somebody. Flattened somebody's tire or laughed at George Kramer and called him "tub o'lard" one time too many. Maybe he reminded Mr. Vickers of Elton Leach. Maybe he called Harry Fredericks "alligator face" one time too often—

Or maybe he met Todd and there was a fight.

"Mom, you don't know how mean Alec was," Kathy said sadly. "Everyone hated him."

"But nobody would have hurt him," Kathy's mother said. She just wouldn't believe anything else.

Kathy stuck her thermos bottle in her lunch bag and headed for school. She wondered if Todd would be there today. She wondered if the police knew about Elton Leach and about the connection between him and Todd.

They had lowered the flag to half-mast at Tyler High. The flag fluttered in the brisk wind. Kathy wondered if anybody really cared that Alec was dead. His parents were sorry, of course, but what about other people?

There were only ninety seniors at Tyler High. Everybody knew everybody else. Kathy couldn't recall a case of a senior ever dying at Tyler. It may have happened years ago. But now one and possibly two seniors had died. Kathy shuddered at the thought.

In chemistry, Mr. Sonderville did not seem upset. He went on with his class as usual. He wrote on the board and talked about next week's test.

"Isn't it terrible about Alec?" a girl

asked. She just wanted to get Mr. Sonderville talking about something other than chemistry.

"We can't waste time talking about news events," Mr. Sonderville said. "We must go over chapter five today."

"I just wondered what you thought," the girl said. "I mean, do you think somebody murdered Alec?"

"I think," Mr. Sonderville said, "that we must go over chapter five today."

The coroner promised her televised news conference at one-thirty. That was right in the middle of Mr. Vickers' history class. "I suppose he'll stop and let us listen," Todd said. "Everybody seems to want to know what happened."

Kathy nodded. "Don't you want to know, Todd?"

"I can't do anything about it. I think I'd rather hear about Charles Sumner and the radical Republicans."

Kathy thought to herself, perhaps you already know what the coroner is going to say. Immediately she hated herself for thinking such a thing. But she couldn't help it.

Mr. Vickers brought in a portable TV set. "I imagine you'll all want to hear what the coroner says," he explained. "So we'll turn this on at one-thirty."

Nobody really listened to the first part of the lecture on Sumner. Everybody was waiting for the conference. There was a great deal of restlessness in the class. Kathy had never seen everybody so nervous and excited.

Mike looked awful. He seemed weak and drained, like he was going to be sick. Kathy had never seen Mike look so bad. Frankly, she was surprised. She knew he had been Alec's friend, but she hadn't realized this thing would hit him so hard. Or maybe it wasn't that at all. Perhaps Mike thought the same thing that had happened to Alec would happen to him.

Maybe those kids taunting him about being "number three" had really gotten to him.

Kathy almost felt sorry for Mike.

At one-thirty, Mr. Vickers turned on the TV, but he didn't seem truly interested in the coroner's report. He began to correct papers. Everybody else stared at the TV screen.

The coroner did not come on right away. First a newsman presented some background on the Ross story. A big picture of Alec was flashed on the screen. Then the reporter read more lies about what a nice kid Alec had been.

Suddenly Kathy heard someone crying. She turned and stared at Mike. His head was down. He was sobbing quietly.

"Oh, Mike," Kathy said sadly.

Mike looked up. "He—he was—my friend—"

Mike wiped his face with his sleeve. Then he seemed embarrassed about crying.

He must have loved Alec, Kathy thought. She had not known they were that close. Even somebody as mean as Alec had a friend who loved him.

The newsman went on and on about

the case. He showed some pictures of the school protest that Mrs. Ross led. He said that a teacher had been forced to leave Tyler High because of that protest. Apparently he was trying to kill time until the coroner arrived.

Suddenly a tall woman with gray hair came into view.

"I believe Dr. Schell is coming into the room," the newsman said. "Yes, yes, it is Dr. Schell. Now we'll find out the cause of death."

Dr. Schell spoke in a low, slow voice. "I will make a brief statement. Following that, I'll take questions." She paused for a moment, then cleared her throat and went on. "The medical examination conducted on the body of Alec Ross revealed that he died of massive head injuries."

Kathy closed her eyes.

The coroner continued, "The back of his head was smashed by a heavy object."

The reporters began to ask questions. "Has the time of death been set?"

"Not yet. But this much I can say: he

was dead before he struck the water."

"No water in his lungs?" A reporter wrote in her notebook.

"No."

"Would you say it was murder?" another reporter asked.

"I cannot go beyond the statement."

Dr. Schell left. The newsman stared into the camera and said, "Well, now we have it. The coroner has just announced that Alec Ross died of head injuries. Dr. Schell stopped short of saying it was murder. But the police homicide department is handling the case at this very moment. Given Dr. Schell's conclusion, there is certainly strong evidence to suspect that Alec Ross, a senior at Tyler High, was murdered. We can only hope that the disappearance of the other missing senior, Dee Loring, is not tied to this tragic case."

Kathy felt numb. She stared at the television screen. Everything was getting blurry before her eyes.

The newsman continued, "Stay tuned at six for more details about the police investigation. Now, back to our regular programming."

Kathy looked at Todd. He showed no emotion. He sat there playing with his pencil.

Most of the other students looked shocked. Mike was crying again.

Dee's desk sat empty. There was writing on the top of her desk. She always wrote on the top of her desk, even though it made the teachers mad.

It made Kathy miserable to look at Dee's desk and to know that she was probably dead, too.

Mr. Vickers turned off the TV set. "Let's just wait for the bell," he said. "No sense in starting class again."

Kathy noticed some police officers standing outside the classroom. She saw Lt. Dexter and two others. They were waiting for the class to end, too. They wanted to talk to someone here!

When the bell rang, it could be the sound of doomsday for someone in this room.

9

LT. DEXTER CALLED out to Mr. Vickers as the students flowed out of the room. "Mr. Vickers, may we see you for a few minutes?"

"Of course," Mr. Vickers said.

Kathy felt like a cold wind was cutting through her body. Todd came up beside her, his face grim. "I wonder what that's about."

"Oh, Todd, maybe they found out about Elton Leach. Maybe they think there's some connection," Kathy said.

"How could they think a man like Mr. Vickers could hurt anybody?" Todd snapped.

"They probably just want to talk to him," Kathy said hopefully.

Mike Perth was standing nearby. He said, "Vickers hated Alec. He always hated Alec. He hates guys with a little spirit."

Kathy turned. "What are you talking about, Mike?"

Mike's eyes were red from crying. "I saw Alec go into Vickers' office the day he disappeared! So I told the cops. I heard Vickers yelling at Alec. And when I looked in the window, I could see Vickers was really mad. He was calling Alec all kinds of names."

"That's a lie!" Todd shouted. "You're lying!"

"Alec was my friend," Mike yelled back. "And I want the cops to get the guy who killed him!"

"Mr. Vickers would never treat anybody like that!" Todd said angrily.

"I heard him!" Mike shouted.

Todd looked like he was about to hit Mike, but he didn't. He just stuffed his hands in his pockets.

"They won't hold Mr. Vickers for something he didn't do," Kathy said softly.

"That jerk!" Todd stormed. "That stupid liar!"

"But, Todd, maybe Mr. Vickers did yell at Alec. It could have happened. It doesn't prove anything."

Todd's face was still twisted with anger. "Why bother Mr. Vickers? All the trouble the poor guy has had. It just isn't fair. Man, the cops sure don't know what they're doing."

"Todd, somebody killed Alec. The police have to talk to everybody—"

Todd stood there a moment in silence. Then he said, "I saw him down by South River that afternoon."

"Who did you see?"

"Alec. I saw him."

Kathy caught her breath. "When?"

"Late. It was getting dark." Todd's hands were shaking.

"Did you—talk to him?"

"Yeah. See, I thought he was going to pull some stupid stunt. I thought he was throwing somebody's books in the river or something. So I asked him what he was doing."

Kathy forced herself to meet Todd's eyes. "Did you fight?"

"We yelled, that's all. I walked away. Alec stayed there. I figured he was meeting somebody."

Todd continued, "Do you know what I think? I think some maniac must have come along. It was probably some guy we don't even know. Maybe he was a drifter. Yeah, I bet that's what happened. Some guy we don't even know came along and killed Alec."

"But why, Todd? That doesn't make sense," Kathy said.

"It doesn't have to make sense," Todd said. "Crazy people do things for no reason."

"But Todd, we've all gone down to South River. I never see guys hanging around. It's not a hangout for drifters."

Todd's hands were still shaking. "Why can't they just forget it?"

"You mean forget that Alec was murdered?"

"Why can't they just say that the world is better off without him?"

"Todd, you're not making any sense! Nobody has the right to kill another person. I don't care what Alec was like. He had a right to live. Nobody had the right to kill him." Kathy felt near tears.

Todd picked up a pebble. He tossed it as far as he could. "Lousy river," he said. "Why didn't it keep him? Why did it have to spit him up again? Maybe even the river hated him and had to spit him out!"

Kathy drew back. Todd seemed so hateful, so full of bitterness and anger. She had hoped he would get over his hatred. She had hoped the scars inside him would heal. But he seemed to be getting worse.

The question burned in her mouth. She had to ask him. She hoped she knew the answer, but she had to ask him.

"Did you—did you do it, Todd? Did you—" Kathy couldn't make herself say it completely. She began to cry. She couldn't wait for his answer. She turned and ran away. Through blinding tears, she climbed on her bike and pedaled home.

Kathy's eyes stung as she rode into the wind. She was so close to believing that Todd had killed Alec.

That night, Kathy couldn't sleep. She kept tossing and turning and having nightmares.

In one nightmare, Kathy was walking along South River. The river was foaming. Kathy knelt at the edge and looked into the river.

"Dee!" she screamed.

Dee was floating, face up, in the river. Her beautiful face would come up and then disappear. Weeds were wrapped around her long, flowing hair. Her eyes were open and staring. "Dee!" Kathy screamed.

Suddenly Todd was standing there. He was smiling and he said, "Can't you see she's dead, Kathy?"

"No," Kathy cried, "she's not dead. Her eyes are open."

He laughed. "That doesn't mean anything. She's dead."

Kathy felt her eyes fill with tears. "She's not dead. Dee! Can you hear me? Tell Todd you aren't dead!"

Dee came up and then disappeared again in the foaming green water.

"They're all going to die," Todd said,

still smiling. "The avenger will strike." He began to chant in a funny, unnatural voice:

"Don't blame the children,
  whatever they do.
Don't blame the children, their world
  is so new.
But I blame the children, and I
  know what to do—"

"Todd, no!" Kathy cried. She knelt at the edge of the river. When Dee came up again, she grabbed for her. She was just inches away. But Kathy couldn't reach her. The weeds were wrapped around Dee's arms like thin, green fingers. The weeds clung to Dee, refusing to let her go.

Dee began to sink into the green foam for the last time.

"Deeeeee!" Kathy screamed.

10

"KATHY!" KATHY'S FATHER was in her bedroom. "What's the matter?"

"Oh, Dad!" Kathy woke up shaking. She was cold all over. "I had this horrible nightmare!"

Kathy's father sat down on her bed and smoothed back her hair. "It's okay, honey. Just take it easy."

It had been years since Kathy had had a really bad nightmare. But she'd never had a nightmare as bad as this one. Tears ran down her face.

"Dad, I was dreaming about Dee Loring. I thought she was in South River. It was so awful. I tried to pull her out of the water but I couldn't . . . Oh, Dad!"

Kathy's father held her in his arms and comforted her. "It's all right, honey. It was just a bad dream. I understand. Terrible things have been happening at school."

"It was so real," Kathy said.

"Come on downstairs and we'll have some hot chocolate."

Kathy followed her father downstairs They were very quiet so they wouldn't wake Kathy's mother.

"Honey," he said as he poured the hot chocolate, "you've been under a lot of pressure lately. I've been worried about you. I don't want to pry into your life, but can I help with anything?"

"I'm worried about Todd," Kathy said as she looked at her father. She trusted him. She knew he would never break a confidence. "Dad, Todd has been so bitter since his accident. And now, since this stuff about Alec and Dee, he seems so strange. He doesn't seem upset about what's happened. He says things like 'it doesn't matter if the police never find out who killed Alec.'"

"Todd has suffered a great deal since that accident. A boy his age is very sensitive about things like scars. I suppose it's not surprising that he feels bitter. Deep down, he's a good boy. I wouldn't worry about him, Kathy. He might say some pretty rough things, but he probably doesn't mean them."

"I told Todd it doesn't matter about the scars. Not to me."

"I know. But Todd has to face those scars himself. He has to know that he can live with what has happened to him. He has to do that himself. You can help him. But he has to do it himself in the end."

Kathy's father dropped a marshmallow in her hot chocolate and continued talking. "Honey, I've known Todd all his life. I know that, deep down, he's a decent young man."

"I guess you're right, Dad." Kathy tried to smile.

In a few minutes, Kathy asked her father, "What do you think happened to Alec, Dad? Who would have killed him?"

"I think it must have been a stranger, Kathy. One of those senseless crimes you read about. It had to be."

"Yes." Kathy wanted to believe that, too. A stranger had killed Alec Ross. Some faceless, nameless stranger. It was no one she liked or loved who had done it. It was a stranger who had struck once or twice and then gone on. It was frightening and sad to think such a person existed, but it was better than thinking Todd had killed Alec.

Kathy went back to bed, but she couldn't sleep. The sky was growing lighter. It was nearly dawn. Soon it would be raining. Large, dark clouds had already blocked the morning sun.

When Kathy left for school, big raindrops were falling.

Todd was waiting for her outside the social studies classroom. "Did you hear?"

"What?"

"They're holding Mr. Vickers for questioning. They dug into his past. They found out about Diane and Elton Leach. They reopened that missing person's case, and now they think maybe Elton's dead, too. They even found out that Mr. Vickers had a nervous breakdown after Diane died." Todd's eyes were filled with fury.

"Kathy, it just makes me sick!"

"I can't believe it," Kathy said.

"Mike told them that junk about hearing Mr. Vickers and Alec fighting. That's one of the big reasons they think Mr. Vickers might have done it. I could take that Mike Perth and knock his head off!"

"Todd, please. Everything is bad enough already. I'm sure the whole thing will be straightened out," Kathy said, although she wasn't really so sure. She didn't feel like going to classes, but she did anyway. She felt like a robot going from room to room. Everything seemed so strange.

All day long, rumors flew around the school. Kids gathered in little groups, whispering. Some of the rumors were very wild.

"Vickers confessed," a girl rushed from English to announce.

"They found Dee's body in South River," a boy yelled on the football field.

It was as if the whole school had gone mad.

When the last bell of the day rang,

Kathy gathered her books and headed for the bike rack. A light drizzle was falling, but she didn't even notice.

She looked around for Todd's truck. It was parked in its usual place. She thought she would ride home with him. Slowly she walked to the truck and piled her bike in the back.

She waited about ten minutes for Todd, but he didn't come. Kathy remembered he had band practice, so she went to the music room. She glanced around at the kids, not spotting Todd.

"Who are you looking for?" the teacher asked.

"Todd Macon."

"He stopped by and said he couldn't wait for band practice tonight. That was about twenty minutes ago."

"Thank you," Kathy said.

Kathy looked around the playing field. Sometimes Todd did some jogging. But the field was empty.

Suddenly Kathy saw a small figure sitting in the rain by the tennis court. She walked over to the slim girl and said, "You're Judy Perth, aren't you? Mike's kid sister."

Judy looked up. "Yeah." The rain was plastering her hair to her face.

"You waiting for somebody, Judy?" Kathy asked.

"Yeah." She looked down and started picking her fingernails.

"You waiting for Mike?"

"Yeah. He said he had to go down to the river." Judy was chewing nervously on her lip. "He was going to have a fight with another boy."

Kathy felt cold terror. "What boy?"

"That Todd Macon," Judy said. "He's mad at Mike for telling that stuff about Mr. Vickers."

"When did Mike leave?"

"About fifteen minutes ago. I wish he'd hurry. He's going to take me home in his car." Judy hung her head.

Kathy rushed down the path that led to South River. All the kids took the same path. It passed between the oaks and then turned right. On it, you could go right down to the river.

Kathy could not stop thinking of Todd. It must have happened this way with Alec, she thought. Todd and Alec had a fight. Maybe Todd had not meant to kill Alec. Maybe the fight had just gotten worse and worse. Maybe it had been an accident that Alec died. Maybe Todd had gotten scared and thrown the body in the river, hoping nobody would find it.

"Todd!" Kathy shouted as she drew near the river. She couldn't see anybody yet. The rain and the mist were like a thick curtain. "Todd!" she cried frantically. She prayed she would be in time.

Suddenly Kathy saw Todd. He was standing near the edge of the river.

Mike was nowhere in sight.

"Todd!" Kathy cried.

The damp, mossy smell of the river rose in a choking fog. Todd's hands were in his pockets. He was staring out at the murky water as if he expected to see something in the dark, cloudy waves.

"Todd," Kathy whispered. She was afraid to ask what he'd done.

He didn't even turn. "Going to be winter, soon," he said. "River will freeze."

Kathy looked around for Mike. She didn't see him.

"Todd, where's Mike?"

He didn't seem to hear her. He looked up at the sky. "Not much good weather left before winter."

Kathy saw Mike then. He was lying in the grass, very still. Kathy wanted to rush to him, but she couldn't move. She looked at Todd and he finally seemed to notice her.

"I had to, Kath," he explained simply. "He was lying about Mr. Vickers. I knew he was lying—Mr. Vickers yelling and screaming at a student. It was a lie. I had to make him tell the truth. I couldn't let Mr. Vickers be blamed for something he didn't do."

Todd's eye was bruised. There was blood on his face. It must have been a terrible fight.

Kathy forced herself to go to Mike. She was afraid to look at him, but she did. His face was bruised, too, but his chest moved up and down. He was breathing!

Kathy dropped to her knees alongside Mike. "Mike, are you okay?"

His eyes snapped open. She saw they were filled with tears. "Alec was my friend," he said.

"I know."

"He asked my sister Judy for a date last week. My sister—she's not very pretty. She's just my sister, but it makes a guy feel bad when nobody asks his sister out—"

Kathy thought about the sad girl sitting in the rain.

"She bought a new outfit for the date, got her hair fixed, and all that kind of stuff. Got some new junk to cover up her face—she looked okay. She was real excited. First time she'd ever been on a date—very first time—"

Mike propped himself up on his elbows. "Only Alec was kidding. It was a joke, see? She waited two hours in the living room. She sat there in her new outfit, just waiting. He called then. He barked into the phone. He asked if the dog was home. He meant my sister. He said Judy was a dog and he wasn't taking no dog out. It was all a joke, the whole date was a joke!"

"What a hateful thing!" Kathy whispered.

The wind was howling and turning cold.

"He was my friend, Alec was. But he shouldn't have done that to Judy. I asked him why he did it. He laughed and said it was the best joke he'd ever pulled. We were—we were standing right here and he laughed and he barked again.

"I told him to stop, but he threw his head back and howled—and I hit him. He fell down the hill. He hit his head on a rock. I got so scared. I pushed him into the river. He was dead already. I was so scared—"

"You killed Alec?" Kathy gasped.

Mike sat up and rested his head on his knees. "I didn't mean to. It was an accident." He began to sob. "He was my friend. I didn't mean to hurt him."

Todd came up suddenly. He knelt down and put his hand on Mike's shoulder. His voice was very soft and there was pity in his eyes. "We know you didn't mean to hurt Alec. Everybody knows that."

Kathy looked at Todd in amazement. He was actually feeling sorry for somebody other than himself! And he was feeling sorry for his old enemy—Mike!

"Come on, Mike," Todd said gently. "We'll tell the police what happened. Everything is going to be okay."

The police listened to Mike's story. It was obviously the truth. They released Mr. Vickers.

Then, the next day, Dee Loring came home. She had been hiding out at a friend's house. Todd had been right all along. She'd been desperate to get her picture in the paper. She'd thought some producer would see her and want to put her in a movie.

Her parents were furious. They even cancelled a surprise trip they'd planned for her to Hawaii. For the first time in Dee's life, her parents really cracked down on her.

On the weekend, the rain stopped. A few days of Indian summer bloomed.

"Busy this Sunday afternoon?" Todd asked Kathy.

"No."

"Want to pack some sandwiches? I'll buy the root beer."

Kathy smiled. "Where are we going?"

"The lake," he grinned. "You know, if it's warm enough, I might even go swimming."

Kathy's face broke into a huge smile. She threw her arms around Todd's neck and he swung her around. "You've got a date," she cried.